Hidden Cherries

Written by *Anne Margaret Lewis* & *Susan Hammon*

Illustrated by Jim DeWildt

Mackinac Island Press

To my husband Brian and my four children, Caitlin, Matthew, Patrick, and Cameron
who are both supportive and inspirational.

Anne Margaret Lewis

To my husband Steve and my sons Evan and Luke, thank you for filling my life
with the best kind of fun and adventure.

Susan Hammon

For my wife Manie and our children, Megan, Amy, Beth and Charley,
they bring laughter and love to me and are the true gifts of life.

Jim DeWildt

Mackinac Island Press and the National Cherry Festival partner together, to make this *Hidden Cherries*,
the first Official Children's Book of the National Cherry Festival. This classic cherry children's book
is sure to be a favorite of generations old and new of the National Cherry Festival.

First Edition

Library of Congress Cataloging-in-Publication Data

Lewis, Anne Margaret, Hammon, Susan, and DeWildt, Jim
Hidden Cherries

Summary: Has anyone seen Mr. Cherry? Mr. Cherry is hiding all over this very cherry book.
Hidden Cherries is overflowing with cherries red and cherries round: find 100 Mr. Cherrys to fill the cherry
pound. When you get done, hunt for more cherry treasures in the cherry treasure box.
ISBN 0-9749145-1-7
Fiction

10 9 8 7 6 5 4 3 2 1

Printed and bound in Canada by Friesens, Altona, Manitoba.

A Mackinac Island Press, Inc. publication

Hidden Cherries

Sweet cherries, tart cherries

Plump cherries, ripe cherries

Cherries red, cherries round

Juicy cherries by the pound

Orchards of cherries to pick by hand

Welcome to our cherry land

Cherry hunting, cherry treasure

Find some cherries for cherry pleasure

I'm Mr. Cherry plump and round
Find **100** of me to make a cherry pour
Turn the page to begin to look
Let's have some fun with this
cherry book

The cherry blessing of the blossoms seen
Cherries marching with the cherry queen
I'm Mr. Cherry plump and round
Find 7 of me to fill your cherry pound

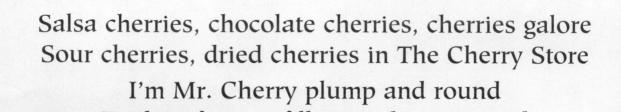

Salsa cherries, chocolate cherries, cherries galore
Sour cherries, dried cherries in The Cherry Store
I'm Mr. Cherry plump and round
Find **8** of me to fill your cherry pound

Good ole cherry shaking and a good ole cherry washing,
Then away on the truck, swishing and sloshing
I'm Mr. Cherry plump and round
Find **10** of me to fill your cherry pound

400 hundred pies baked, 400 hundred pies sold
Would you like your cherry pie....a la mode?
I'm Mr. Cherry plump and round
Find **9** of me to fill your cherry pound

Bears and otters and beavers too
Find some cherries at the Clinch Park Zoo
I'm Mr. Cherry plump and round
Find **10** of me to fill your cherry pound

Pie after pie, bite after bite
The pie eating contest is a very cherry sight
I'm Mr. Cherry plump and round
Find **7** of me to fill your cherry pound

Grab a cherry and find the pit
Lean way back...get ready...spit
I'm Mr. Cherry plump and round
Find **7** of me to fill your cherry pound

Black cherry, cherry chip dripping off your face
Eating cherry ice cream at your favorite place
I'm Mr. Cherry plump and round
Find 8 of me to fill your cherry pound

Cherries light and cherries dark
Pick some cherries, some sweet, some tart
I'm Mr. Cherry plump and round
Find 9 of me to fill your cherry pound

Cherry cobbler and cherry jam
Would you like some cherries, Ma'am?
I'm Mr. Cherry plump and round
Find **6** of me to fill your cherry pound

Cherry chill and cherry freeze
Winter blows a cherry chill breeze
I'm Mr. Cherry plump and round
Find **6** of me to fill your cherry pound

Cherry picnic and cherry pies
Open the basket for a cherry surprise
I'm Mr. Cherry plump and round
Find **6** of me to fill your cherry pound

Michigan cherries sweet and
Michigan cherries sour
Millions of cherries in Michigan for everyone to devour
I'm Mr. Cherry plump and round
Find **7** of me to fill your cherry pound

Now you've found 100 Mr. Cherrys to make a cherry pound
Go back to each page and search for cherry treasures...
in the cherry lost and found.

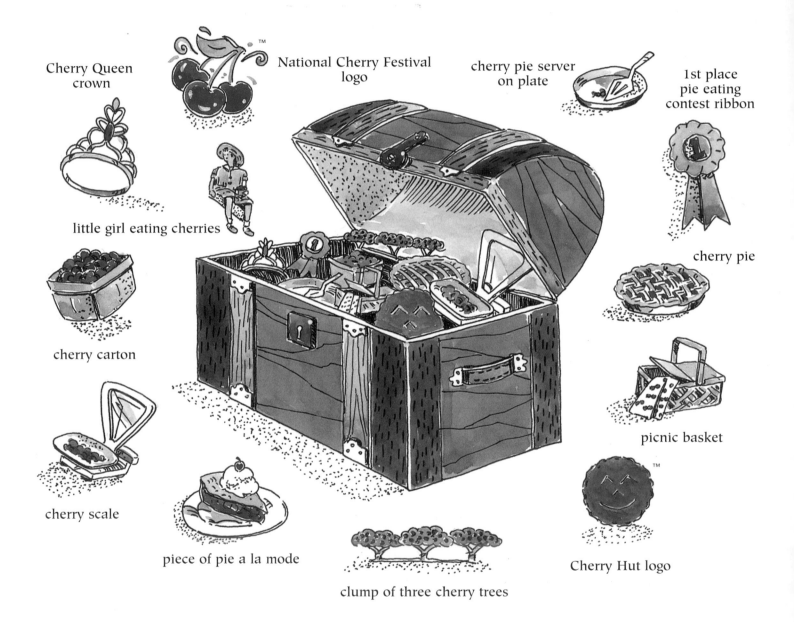

Cherry Queen crown

National Cherry Festival logo

cherry pie server on plate

1st place pie eating contest ribbon

little girl eating cherries

cherry pie

cherry carton

picnic basket

cherry scale

piece of pie a la mode

clump of three cherry trees

Cherry Hut logo